What the World Could Make

A Story of Hope

written by
Holly M. McGhee

illustrated by
Pascal Lemaître

Roaring Brook Press
New York

The friends thought it a wonder—
winter white flakes a gift from the sky.

They let them land . . .
the snow melting against their warmth.
The friends could sit there always,
just like that—

watching what the world could make.

"Isn't it beautiful?" said Bunny.
The other watched the snowflakes fall.
"Yes," said Rabbit.

"I wish it would snow forever," Bunny said.

"Forever?" asked Rabbit. "For always?"

"No . . . not exactly. Not that kind of forever."

"I think I know," Rabbit said.
"You mean the kind of forever
where you remember it even after it ends?"

Rabbit stood up
and began
to make . . .
a snowball.
A snowball for Bunny.
With a snowball—round as their tails
and big as their friendship—
Bunny would remember the snow
for forever . . .

With each turn, the snowball
got bigger
and bigger
and bigger,
until Rabbit knew it was ready.

"This is for you," said Rabbit,
"so you can remember forever."

"For me?" Bunny asked.
"You made a gift from the heart
with a gift from the sky!"

The friends thought it a wonder,
lilacs in spring beginning to bloom.
Tiny clusters of flowers—
purple, dark and light,
fuchsia and white.

"I like their colors," said Rabbit.
Bunny breathed in the blossoms.
"I like their smell."

"I wish they would bloom forever,"
said Rabbit.
"Forever?" Bunny asked. "For always?"
"No . . . not exactly. Not that kind of forever."

"I know what you mean," said Bunny this time. "The kind of forever where you remember it even after it ends!"

Bunny made a crown,
weaving together the branches and flowers,
until it was ready for Rabbit . . .

"This is for you," Bunny said.
"So you can remember forever."

"It fits!" said Rabbit.
"You made a gift from the heart
with a gift from the earth—for me!"

The friends thought it a wonder,
summer—

sea pickles in the marsh,
bright green and salty.

"Let's take a bite," Bunny said.
"Okay," said Rabbit.
Wet and crunchy,
briny and tart.

"They're yummy!" said Rabbit.
Bunny finished one, then another.
"Delicious!"
"A gift to us," said Rabbit.
"From the sun and the sea and the sand."

The friends thought it a wonder
what the autumn world could make—
a ginkgo carpet to behold . . .

They wished they could keep it forever,
this magical kingdom of gold.

Then Rabbit gathered the leaves in a pile

and said to Bunny, "JUMP!"

And Bunny said to Rabbit, "JUMP!"

So Bunny jumped, and Rabbit did too,

and they jumped

and jumped

and jumped!

Celebrating . . .

d could make!

And then—
the snow began to fall . . . again.
"It's snowing," Rabbit whispered.

It was a wonder,
white flakes coming down,
the friends together,
watching . . .
anew . . .

what the world could make.